Hello, Family Members,

Learning to read is one of the most important ~~of~~ of early childhood. **Hello Reader!** books are ~~designed~~ to help children become skilled readers who like to read. Beginning readers learn to read by remembering frequently used words like "the," "is," and "and"; by using phonics skills to decode new words; and by interpreting picture and text clues. These books provide both the stories children enjoy and the structure they need to read fluently and independently. Here are suggestions for helping your child *before*, *during*, and *after* reading:

Before
- Look at the cover and pictures and have your child predict what the story is about.
- Read the story to your child.
- Encourage your child to chime in with familiar words and phrases.
- Echo read with your child by reading a line first and having your child read it after you do.

During
- Have your child think about a word he or she does not recognize right away. Provide hints such as "Let's see if we know the sounds" and "Have we read other words like this one?"
- Encourage your child to use phonics skills to sound out new words.
- Provide the word for your child when more assistance is needed so that he or she does not struggle and the experience of reading with you is a positive one.
- Encourage your child to have fun by reading with a lot of expression . . . like an actor!

After
- Have your child keep lists of interesting and favorite words.
- Encourage your child to read the books over and over again. Have him or her read to brothers, sisters, grandparents, and even teddy bears. Repeated readings develop confidence in young readers.
- Talk about the stories. Ask and answer questions. Share ideas about the funniest and most interesting characters and events in the stories.

I do hope that you and your child enjoy this book.

—Francie Alexander
Reading Specialist,
Scholastic's Learning Ventures

To my parents, who made every holiday fun
—K.K.

For Stevie
—B.D.

**Go to www.scholastic.com for Web site information
on Scholastic authors and illustrators.**

Text copyright © 1999 by Kathleen Keeler.
Illustrations copyright © 1999 by Bob Doucet.
All rights reserved. Published by Scholastic Inc.
SCHOLASTIC, HELLO READER, CARTWHEEL BOOKS and associated logos
are trademarks and/or registered trademarks of Scholastic Inc.

Library of Congress Cataloging-in-Publication Data available.

ISBN 0-439-09855-6

12 11 10 9 8 7 6 5 4 3 2   9/9 0/0 01 02 03 04

Printed in the U.S.A.   24
First printing, October 1999

I DARE YOU

Stories to Scare You

by Kathleen Keeler
Illustrated by Bob Doucet

Hello Reader! — Level 3

SCHOLASTIC INC.
New York   Toronto   London   Auckland   Sydney
Mexico City   New Delhi   Hong Kong

This is a test. Read these three stories . . . if you dare. Only the brave will keep reading to the end. Will you?

The Cemetery

Kate was ready to go trick-or-treating.

Screech. She opened her front door.

Her white cat, Luna, ran out.

Out into the rain.

Out into the thunder.

Out into the lightning.

"Luna," Kate called. "Here, kitty."

Luna kept running.

Kate ran after her.

She followed Luna's white tail
around the corner.

"Here, Luna. Here, kitty," Kate called.

Luna kept running.

Kate followed Luna's white tail
into an alley.

"Here, Luna. Here, kitty," she called.

Luna kept running.

Kate followed Luna's white tail
up to a big, black gate.
"Here, Luna," she called.
"Come out of the cemetery."
Luna kept running.

Kate took one step inside the gate.

She saw something white.

She touched it.

"Eeek!"

It was not her cat!

Lightning lit up the sky.

"Whew!" It was just a flower.

Kate took another step.

Again, she saw something white.

She touched it.

"Eeek!"

It was not her cat!

Lightning lit up the sky.

"Whew!" It was just a stone bench.

Kate took one more step.

Once again, she saw something white.

She touched it.

"Eeek!"

It was not her cat!

Lightning lit up the sky.

"Whew!" It was just a tombstone!

Kate tried to run away.

But her feet got tangled up in something.

"YOWL!"

What was that?

Lightning lit up the sky.
It was Luna!
But now Luna was all black.
Halloween magic had turned Luna
into a black cat!

The thunder thumped.
The lightning cracked.
The rain raged.
Kate could not leave Luna there.
She grabbed her cat and ran.
She ran back across the cemetery.
She ran back down the alley.
She ran back around the corner.

She ran inside her house.

"Mom! Mom!" Kate screamed.

Her mom ran to the hall.

"What is it?" her mom asked.

Kate held Luna up.

"Oh, poor Luna is all wet," Kate's mom said.

Kate looked down.

Luna was all wet and . . .

ALL WHITE!

All except one small spot of black mud
still on her tail.

Bet you were scared. No? Well, that was just a warm-up. Try reading the next story . . . if you dare!

Home Scary Home

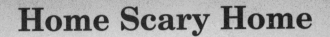

It was Halloween night.

Ben and Clare were trick-or-treating.

They walked down a dark street.

Ben did not like it.

But he did not tell Clare.

She might laugh.

They walked under swishing trees.

Ben did not like it.

But he did not tell Clare.

She might laugh.

A ghost jumped out at them.
"BOO!"
Ben did not like it one bit.
But he did not tell Clare.
She might laugh.
Ben was glad he was almost home.

"Bye, Clare," Ben said.
He started to run.
Into his yard.
Up his front steps.
Through his door.
Home at last!

"*BOO!*"
That was loud.
That was *inside* his house.
Ben held his breath.

"*BOO!*"

He heard it again.

It was coming from his kitchen.

He walked down the dark hall.

Ben did not like it.

"*BOO!*"

He turned the dark corner.

Ben did not like it.

"*BOO!*"

He tiptoed up to the kitchen door.
Ben did not like it one bit.
"BOO! BOO! BOO!"

Ben had to do something.
He closed his eyes.
He yelled as loud as he could.
He hurled himself through the kitchen door.
"*AHHHHH!*" his dad screamed.
"*AHHHHH!*" his mom screamed.

Then his mom smiled.

"You did it, Ben!

You scared away my hiccups.

Dad saying *'Boo!'* was not scary enough."

Ben could not wait to tell Clare.

She would laugh.

You must be scared by now. No? Well, you are not done yet. You still have to read the scariest story of all . . . if you dare!

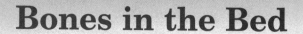

Bones in the Bed

It was Halloween night.

Dave was ready to go trick-or-treating.

Elroy sniffed at his dog door.

He wanted to go, too.

"Okay," said Dave, "but you have to be scary. It *is* Halloween, you know."

Elroy did not know about Halloween.

But he did know about being scary.

He was scary to cats.

He was scary to ducks.

He was scary to the mailman.

Elroy growled.

"Good dog," said Dave.

Dave and Elroy went to the first house.

"Trick-or-treat," said Dave.

"Grrrr-Grrrr," said Elroy,
showing his scary teeth.

Dave got a candy.
Elroy did not get a bone.
He did not get anything.
That is not fair! thought Elroy.

They went to the next house.

"Trick-or-treat," said Dave.

"Grrrr-Grrrr," said Elroy,

showing his scary teeth again.

Dave got another candy.

Elroy still did not get a bone.

He did not get anything.

That is so mean! thought Elroy.

They went to the next house.

"Trick-or-treat," said Dave.

"Grrrr-Grrrr," said Elroy,

showing his scary teeth again.

Dave got more candy.

Elroy did not get a bone.

Not even a small one.

He did not get anything.

This stinks! thought Elroy.

They went to all the houses on both sides
of the street.

All the houses except the dark, spooky house.

Dave got lots of candy.

Elroy did not get anything.

It was time to go home.
But Elroy would not stop until
he got some bones.
He would go to that dark, spooky house.
He would growl for bones there.

When Dave got home, he ate ten candies
and went to bed.
Soon Elroy came home, too.
Elroy dropped something cold in the bed.
He dropped another cold thing in the bed.
He dropped lots of cold things in the bed.
"What are these things?" Dave wondered.
He snapped on the light.

"*AAAAAAH!*" Dave screamed.

There were bones in his bed!

Lots of bones!

Arm bones!

Leg bones!

"*AAAAAAAAAH!*"

Dave ran to tell his dad.

"You just ate too much candy," said his dad.

"You can sleep in here."

Dave jumped in and pulled the covers
over his head.

He knew he had seen bones.

Lots of bones!

Arm bones!

Leg bones!

He would never go back to his room again.

In Dave's room, Elroy liked having
the bed to himself.
He had lots of room to eat his bones.
He started to chew on an arm bone.
Yuck! Spit-spit-spooey.
This bone was plastic.

Then he started to chew on a leg bone.
Yuck! Spit-spit-spooey.
This bone was plastic, too.

He bit all the bones.
All of these bones were plastic!
Elroy jumped down.
He ran out his dog door.
He ran back to the spooky house.

The skeleton was still hanging
on the door. He bit the rest of the bones.
Yuck! Spit-spit-spooey.
All of these bones were plastic, too!
There sure are a lot of scary surprises on
Halloween night, thought Elroy.

Admit it! You were scared that
time, right? No? You are very brave.
Brave enough to go outside
on Halloween night!